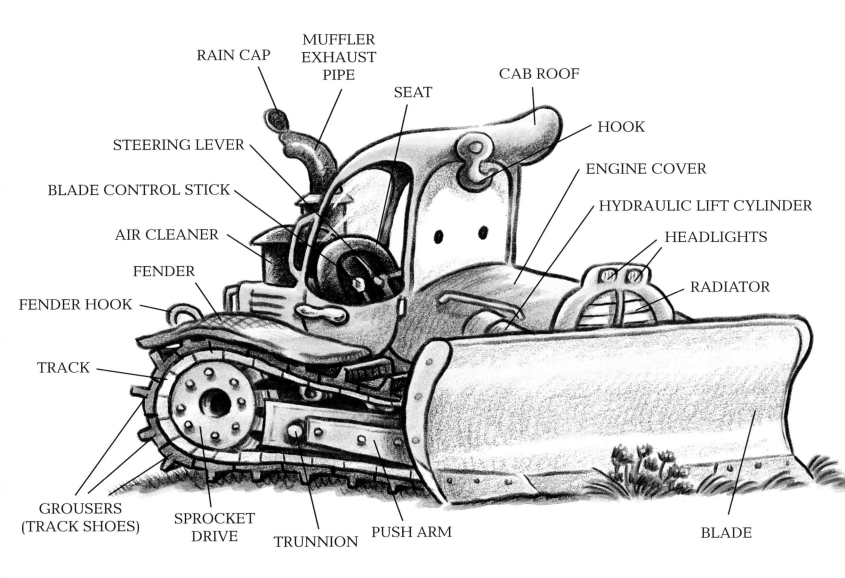

RAIN CAP

MUFFLER
EXHAUST
PIPE

SEAT

CAB ROOF

HOOK

STEERING LEVER

ENGINE COVER

BLADE CONTROL STICK

HYDRAULIC LIFT CYLINDER

AIR CLEANER

HEADLIGHTS

FENDER

RADIATOR

FENDER HOOK

TRACK

GROUSERS
(TRACK SHOES)

SPROCKET
DRIVE

TRUNNION

PUSH ARM

BLADE

For Marlene

Copyright © 1996 by Rick Meyerowitz. All rights reserved under International and Pan-American Copyright Conventions.
Published in the United States by Random House, Inc., New York, and simultaneously in Canada by Random House of Canada Limited, Toronto.
http://www.randomhouse.com/
Library of Congress Cataloging-in-Publication Data:
Meyerowitz, Rick, 1943–. Elvis the bulldozer / written and illustrated by Rick Meyerowitz.
p. cm. SUMMARY: After a terrible accident in the garden where he works, Elvis the bulldozer is banished to the garbage dump
until he proves himself a hero and returns to the garden he loves.
ISBN: 0-679-86958-1 [1. Bulldozers—Fiction. 2. Construction equipment—Fiction. 3. Gardens—Fiction.] I. Title.
PZ7.M571554E1 1996 [E]—dc20 95-12189
Printed in the United States of America 10 9 8 7 6 5 4 3 2 1

ELVIS THE BULLDOZER

WRITTEN AND ILLUSTRATED BY

RICK MEYEROWITZ

RANDOM HOUSE 🏠 NEW YORK

I n the cool of the morning, Elvis the bulldozer rumbled out of his shed in the big garden.

"Good morning, Elvis," said Iris. "Ready for a hard day's work?"

"Of course he's ready!" said Rusty. "He's the hardest-working bulldozer there ever was."

Rusty kept Elvis tuned and oiled. Elvis's trim sparkled, and his fresh paint gleamed golden and buttery. There wasn't a speck of rust on him. Elvis was the best-looking, best-running bulldozer on two treads.

Elvis spun his sprockets. He loved his friends, and he loved his work.

"Today," Iris said, "we're going to dig a pond by the waterfall. There are some heavy rocks to move."

Elvis revved his engine and honked. If Iris asked him to, he would move a mountain. Wasn't he the hardest-working bulldozer there ever was?

The cherry orchard was Elvis's favorite place. From here, he could see the white arbors of the rose garden and the great glass conservatory glistening in the sun. Elvis idled, filling his carburetors with the sweet smell of cherry blossoms. He sighed, then gave a gentle honk. Iris and Rusty blinked and stirred. The orchard cast a peaceful spell, but they had work to do.

Elvis loved the smell of fresh earth. He loved
digging his treads deep in it, and lifting
stumps and gnarled roots from it.
Most of all, he loved digging
up big old rocks. By
afternoon, Elvis
had made a
huge pile of
round rocks.
He sat
happily
on top,
surveying
his work.
Then he
looked
out over
the garden
wall. To his
surprise, he
saw a great
parade of building machines
roaring down the road. What a noise they made!

Growling dump trucks led the way, followed by backhoes with
ripper claws. There were excavators and crushers, scrapers
and grapple skidders. There were graders and compactors,
and low wide-mouthed pavers, whose hot asphalt boiled
and cooked like black oatmeal. Then came rollers,
as dignified and slow-moving as hippos. And
there were bulldozers, too, of all sorts.

Above the tumult, Elvis heard them singing this song:

We're the machines that people made
To flatten meadow and uproot glade.
We think not of nature, we cannot be slowed.
We're mighty machines, we're building a road—
And we love it! We love it!

Elvis felt a thrill surge through his valves. A powerful young crusher called out, "Knock down the wall, brother. Join us! We're building the big roads and traveling them to see the world."

Oil rushed to his pan. Elvis felt giddy, and his blade trembled. "Why, I could build the big roads, too!" he thought. "I could travel them and see the wide world."

"Elvis," Iris said, "you're daydreaming."
"Daydreaming?" said Rusty. "Not our Elvis.
He's the hardest-working bulldozer
there ever was. Why, he could move
a mountain if he wanted to."
Elvis's valves swelled. Let
others follow the road
outside. All his paths
were here in the
garden. He
turned so quickly
on his tracks that the rocks
on his pile shifted. One rock
rolled off. Another followed.
Elvis slid backward. The
pile he had so carefully built
came apart like a mountain of
marbles. Rocks fell in every
direction. A large one bounced
into his cab and wedged his
throttle into reverse. Elvis
couldn't steer…and
he couldn't stop!

He skidded past the newly dug pond and down the hill, tearing up the rhododendrons, uprooting the sunflowers, charging through the marigolds, and crushing the rose arbors. Helpless to stop himself, he roared backward at full speed toward the great glass conservatory.

Iris and Rusty ran after him, but there was nothing they could do. With a noise like the breaking of a thousand dinner plates, he crashed into the conservatory, sending glass and plants flying.

When everything had settled, there was Elvis, windshield deep in the lily pool, looking very unhappy.

The garden managers came running. "That bulldozer has to go!" they demanded.

"But it wasn't his fault," Iris cried.

"It was an accident," added Rusty.

But the managers didn't want to hear it. "He has to go," they said. The next day, they sold him to roadbuilders.

That evening in the shed, Rusty dried Elvis's plugs and poked at his vents. Iris sat in Elvis's cab, keeping him company through the long, sad night.

At dawn, Elvis was loaded onto a flatbed truck. Rusty opened Elvis's engine panel and placed a handful of cherry blossoms inside. "Don't forget us," he whispered.

"We won't forget you," Iris said tearfully.

The big truck rumbled slowly through the iron gates. They clanged shut, and Elvis was carried away from the people, the garden, and the life he loved.

He was hauled to a vast construction site. There, giant scrapers pawed the ground. Huge backhoes ripped at rocks. Big bulldozers raced their engines, ready for a hard day's work.

As the newest member of the company, Elvis was given the chance to show what he could do—flattening and clearing a large field. Elvis was a roadbuilder now, and he would be a good one.

He rumbled off,
leading the other bulldozers. And as
they thundered along, they growled this song:

A bulldozer bulls, and a bulldozer dozes.
So get out of our way, we don't smell like roses.
Don't try to wash us, 'cause we don't like hoses.
We live in the dirt, wear mud like a shirt—
And we love it! We love it!

When they arrived at the field, Elvis stopped short. There must be some mistake! This was a magnificent old cherry orchard with more than a hundred trees in full bloom.

Elvis ground his gears. He dug in his grousers and locked his brakes. He wouldn't—he couldn't—destroy this beautiful cherry orchard.

"Do your job!" yelled the builders. "Flatten that field. You're a bulldozer. Now bulldoze!"

Elvis wouldn't budge. The builders jumped up and down. They kicked him. Nothing they could do or say would make Elvis move.

Finally, the men gave up. They ordered the other bulldozers to begin pushing down the trees. The earth shook with the roar of machines and the sound of splintering wood.

As the old orchard fell, a blizzard of cherry blossoms filled the air. Some settled on Elvis's bonnet. A tear ran down his windscreen.

The builders had Elvis towed away. He was sold, and then sold again. He was moved from place to place until he no longer knew where he was. Finally, he was sold to the Renegade Road Company, where he was given the meanest, lowest job they could give a bulldozer that wouldn't bulldoze: hauling trash.

Day followed day. Summer and fall went by, and winter came. It snowed. Sometimes his gears froze.

His oil needed changing. He coughed black smoke and sputtered. His paint wore off. No one took care of him. He became grimy and rusty. Once he had thought he could move a mountain. Now the only mountain he could move was one of trash.

One drizzly morning in early spring, Elvis heard the builders arguing with a woman. "Please don't build your road across the hillside," she was saying. "You'll destroy the beautiful old forest. Those trees have roots that hold the hill together."

Elvis knew that voice. It was Iris!

The roadbuilders said, "Stop work? Just because of a few trees?"

"But it's not just 'a few trees.' What you do on that hillside affects all the land around it. Without the trees, the earth will wash away with the first big rain," Iris warned. "That hill supports the dam, and the dam holds back the reservoir."

But the builders wouldn't listen. "Nothing can stop us," they said. "When we meet a river, we bridge it. When we come to a mountain, we blast it. Why should we go around a forest when we can cut through it?" Elvis wanted to go to Iris, but he thought she would be angry with him for being part of the Renegade Road Company. So he trundled away with the trash. He didn't notice Iris turn and look for a long moment at him, a grimy, rusty bulldozer pushing trash through the mud.

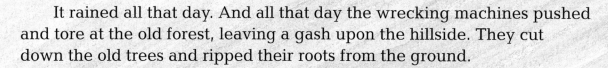

It rained all that day. And all that day the wrecking machines pushed and tore at the old forest, leaving a gash upon the hillside. They cut down the old trees and ripped their roots from the ground.

On the other side of the hill lay the enormous reservoir. Like a bathtub with too much in it, it began to overflow. Water splashed over the top, mixing with the earth just loosened from the grip of ancient roots. It became a flood of mud and rock. Heavy machines began to slip and slide. Excavators lost their grip on the hillside; scrapers and bulldozers went tumbling and skidding in the mud.

Alone in his shed, Elvis shifted gears uneasily as he listened to the rain rattling on the tin roof. Suddenly, a gust of wind blew open the side door. Two people came in.

"You were right," said the taller one. "It's him."

"Elvis!" they cried. "Oh, Elvis, we've finally found you."

It was Iris and Rusty! They climbed his fenders, laughing and crying. Elvis pumped his pistons with joy.

Outside, they could hear the roar and skittering of machines in the mud and the splashing footsteps of many men.

"Run for your lives!" the men yelled. "The dam is going to break."

"C'mon, Elvis," said Rusty. "We've got a job for the strongest, hardest-working bulldozer there ever was."

Elvis fired up his engine. He felt his old strength surge through him, right down to his smallest bolt. He was ready to move a real mountain!

With a mighty leap, he burst through the shed doors. The rain was beating down. Thunder and lightning crashed. Men ran this way and that. A scraper, on its side in the mud, spun its huge wheels helplessly. Heavy trucks collided with each other in their mad stampede away from the weakened hillside.

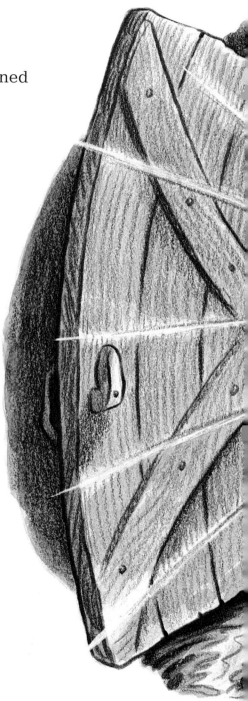

Elvis fought his way past them all, struggling uphill. He *had* to stop the dam from breaking. People were in the town below. Children were in their beds. There were schools and parks. The garden was there—*his* garden!—and the cherry orchard. He wasn't going to let anything happen to his orchard.

Cut logs lay strewn about. He set to work gathering and piling them against the dam.

He pushed and shoved the mighty logs upward. Lightning crackled and thunder boomed. But he kept working all through the long night.

By dawn the rain had stopped. People began to arrive from the town. They climbed, cautiously at first, then faster, as they saw that it was safe. They clambered over slippery rocks and overturned trees until, at last, they reached the hilltop.

There they found a mountain of thick logs and damp earth wedged against the dam, holding it in place. Sitting at the very top of the mountain was Elvis the bulldozer, keeping watch over his night's work.

The strongest, hardest-working bulldozer there ever was had moved a mountain and saved the town.

The builders fixed the dam and replanted the hillside.

The managers welcomed Elvis back to the garden. Once Iris and Rusty finished painting him, Elvis looked better than ever.

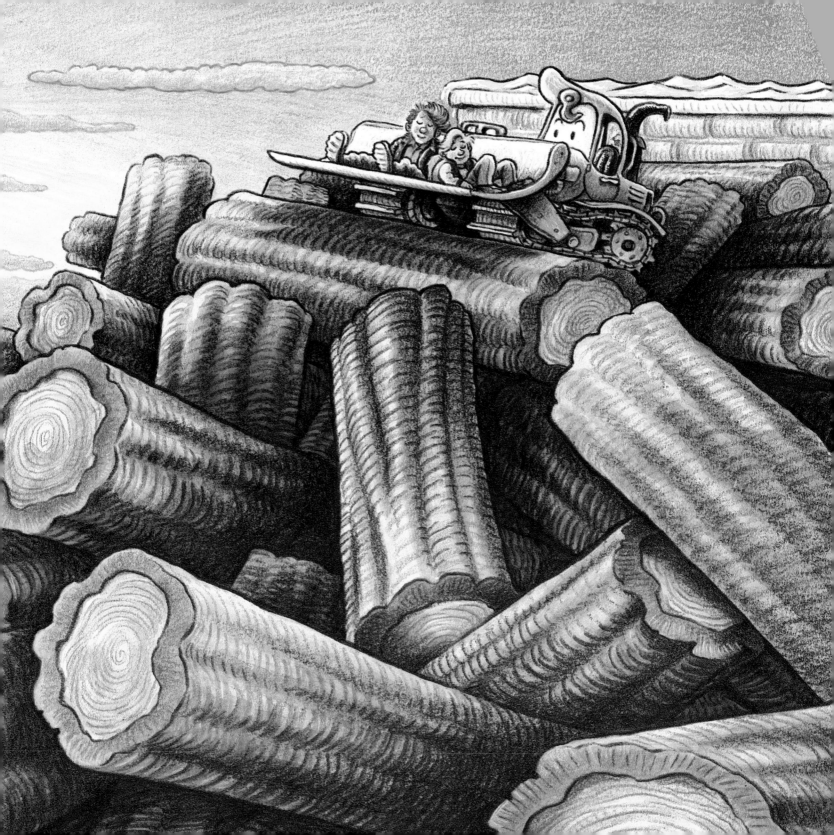

And that's where Elvis remains to this day. He's hard at work tending the flowers and shaded paths, or sitting under the sun-dappled boughs of the cherry orchard, his engine purring softly, on a bright spring afternoon.